A HOME IN THE WOODS
FOR
LADDIE AND PIPER

Laddie and Piper, have just come home from their honeymoon in Europe. Oh, what a grand time they had there. Now they are back in their tiny apartment and oh how they wanted a home of their own.

The mailman came early the next morning and Laddie went out to see what mail they had received. He opened a letter and read it to Piper. The letter read:

Dear Laddie and Piper,

Welcome home from your trip to Europe. I have good news for you. I am giving you a home in the woods. I know you have been wanting this for a long time. This is my wedding present to both of you. I hope you will be so happy there. To find it, walk to the park near your home and look for a long path, into the woods. You won't get lost, for God has placed a lot of His creatures there, to guide you along the way.

With much love,

Aunt Molly

After a good night's sleep and a quick breakfast, Laddie and Piper started on the great adventure of finding their new home.

They walked to the park just as the sun, the sky and the meadow were beginning to wake up. They soon found the path they were to take to find their home and just as Aunt Molly's letter said, "there was a beautiful creature, a golden horse, who was ready to tell them the way they should go." The horse said "keep going along this path and there will be a gentle doe for you to talk to." They thanked the horse, for his help.

It was late afternoon, when they rested again. They walked off the path, to look at a beautiful meadow. As they were admiring the beauty of it, along came a gentle doe. They asked her if she knew the way to their new home. The doe said, "she had seen it once and knew it was along the path." Just keep going and you will see a beautiful swan. Maybe she knows. Laddie and Piper thanked the doe for her kindness and kept going along the path.

As they went along the path, they decided to rest under the shade of the tree that was standing right by the lake. Soon, a swan came swimming towards them. Oh, she was so graceful as she swam along. Laddie and Piper called out to her. They asked her if she knew the way to their new home. The stately swan answered "I'm sure if you continue along this path, you will find your home. You will have a few more hills to climb first. But I know it is in the forest, somewhere."

It was getting to be evening, but these two Scotties kept walking. At first, they didn't see the bunny, who was watching them, but soon they heard the bunny make a squeaking sound, that seemed to say to them, "just keep going." You will find your home soon.

As they walked, they noticed all the beautiful fireflies. They seemed to be guiding Laddie and Piper and they certainly lit up the way that the Scotties should go. They stopped to rest, at the top of the hill.

They could not believe their eyes and they looked at each other as if to say. "Can this be real?   Is this our new home?" You can imagine how quickly they ran down the hill?

They got to the door of the home, which was really a beautiful tree house. They could see the fireflies had lit a path to that door and even filled the lantern, so they could read the sign on the door, which read: WELCOME HOME! "Could this truly be our new home?" Laddie knocked on the door. No one answered, but his knocking caused the door to swing open. It opened as if to say, "This is your home, come on in".

One firefly lit the candle on the kitchen window sill. Laddie and Piper had fun, as they looked around their new home. They just couldn't believe how perfect it was, just what they had always wanted.

Just like any Scottie would, they headed to the kitchen. Food and fresh water were waiting for them. By now, they were very tired and soon went to bed.

Morning came! Laddie woke up first. He was heading upstairs, to explore the attic. Piper soon followed.

What fun they had, looking all around. Laddie noticed
the tri-cycle Aunt Molly must have ridden, when she was
a girl. There was a picture on the wall, of their Aunt Moly
too. Piper was busy playing dress up with all the
old-styled clothing Aunt Molly had left there.

They were so grateful to their Aunt, who loved them so much and thanked God, for their new home. Piper told Laddie how much she loved it there and that she would like them to live there forever. Of course they wrote Aunt Molly a letter thanking her for her wonderful gift to them. They then took a walk to thank all of God's creatures for helping them find their new home.

Within a few days, Laddie and Piper walked to their old home and said "good bye" to all of their old friends. They invited their friends to come visit them. They told them "just go to the park and look for the long path that leads into the forest and that God's creatures will show them the way."

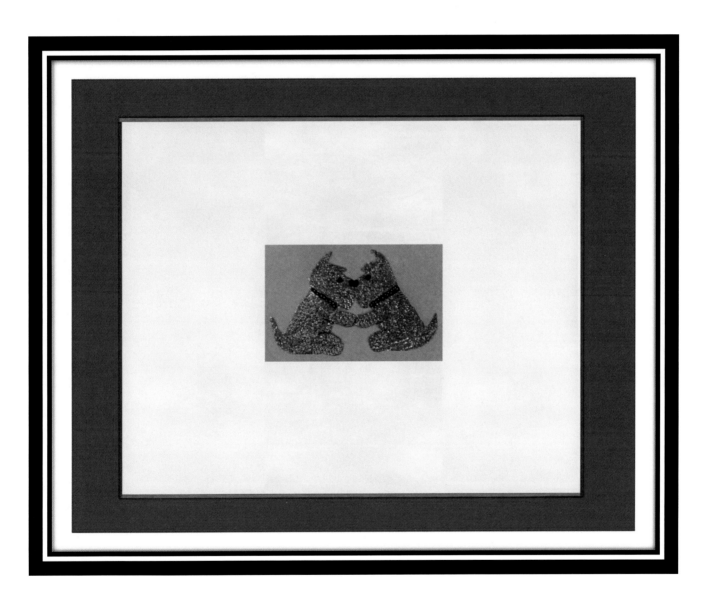

HAPPY

TAILS

ENDING!